Table of Contents:

Scary Stories To Tell In The Dark:

Chapter No 1: The Red Room

"I can assure you," said I," that it'll take a veritably palpable ghost to scarify me." And I stood up before the fire with my glass in my hand.

"It's your own picking," said the man with the withered arm, and glanced at me mistrustfully.

"Eight- and- twenty times," said I," I've lived, and noway a ghost have I seen as yet."

The old woman sat gaping hard into the fire, her pale eyes wide open." Ay," she broke in;" and eight- and- twenty times you have lived and noway seen the likes of this house, I reckon. There is a numerous effects to see, when one's still but eight- and- twenty." She swayed her head sluggishly from side to side." A numerous effects to see and anguish for."

I half suspected the old people were trying to enhance the spiritual demons of their house by their droning asseveration. I put down my empty glass on the table and looked about the room, and caught a regard of myself, shortened and broadened to an insolvable soundness, in the queer old glass at the end of the room." Well," I said," if I see anything to-night, I shall be so much the wiser. For I come to the business with an open mind."

"It's your own picking," said the man with the withered arm formerly more.

I heard the sound of a stick and a shambling step on the flags in the passage outdoors, and the door creaked on its hinges as a alternate old man entered, more fraudulent, more wrinkled, further aged indeed than the first. He supported himself by a single bolsterer, his eyes were covered by a shade, and his lower lip, half prevented, hung pale and pink from his decaying unheroic teeth. He made straight for an arm- president on the contrary side of the table, sat down clumsily, and began to cough. The man with the withered arm gave this new- adventurer a short regard of positive dislike; the old woman took no notice of his appearance, but remained with her eyes fixed steadily on the fire.

"I said-- it's your own picking," said the man with the withered arm, when the coughing had desisted for a while.

"It's my own picking," I answered.

The man with the shade came apprehensive of my presence for the first time, and threw his head back for a moment and sideways, to see me. I caught a evanescent regard of his eyes, small and bright and lit. Also he began to cough and expectorate again.

"Why do not you drink?" said the man with the withered arm, pushing the beer towards him. The man with the shade poured out a glassful with a shaky hand that splashed half as much again on the deal table. A monstrous shadow of him squinched upon the wall and mocked his action as he poured and drank. I must confess I had scarce anticipated these grotesque custodians. There's to my mind commodity inhuman in caducity, commodity hunkering and atavistic; the mortal rates feel to drop from old people insensibly day by day. The three of them made me feel uncomfortable, with their haggard silences, their fraudulent carriage, their apparent unfriendliness to me and to one another.

still," said I," you will show me to this haunted room of yours," If."

The old man with the cough jerked his head back so suddenly that it startled me, and shot another regard of his red eyes at me from under the shade; but no bone answered me. I awaited a nanosecond, glancing from one to the other.

still," I said a little louder," if you'll show me to this haunted room of yours," If."

"There is a candle on the arbor outside the door," said the man with the withered arm, looking at my bases as he addressed me." But if you go to the red room to- night----"

"This night of all nights!" said the old woman.

"You go alone."

"Veritably well," I answered." And which way do I go?"

"You go along the passage for a bit," said he," until you come to a door, and through that's a helical staircase, and half- way up that's a wharf and another door covered with baize. Go through that and down the long corridor to the end, and the red room is on your left up the way."

"Have I got that right?" I said, and repeated his directions. He corrected me in one particular.

"And are you really going?" said the man with the shade, looking at me again for the third time, with that queer, unnatural tilting of the face.

("This night of all nights!" said the old woman.)

"It's what I came for," I said, and moved towards the door. As I did so, the old man with the shade rose and staggered round the table, so as to be near to the others and to the fire. At the door, I turned and looked at them, and saw they were each close together, dark against the firelight, gaping at me over their shoulders, with an intent expression on their ancient faces.

"Good- night," I said, setting the door open.

"It's your own picking," said the man with the withered arm.

I left the door wide open until the candle was well alight, and also I shut them in and walked down the chilly, echoing passage.

I must confess that the oddness of these three old pensioners in whose charge her baroness had left the castle, and the deep- toned, old- fashioned cabinetwork of the char's room in which they convened, affected me in malignancy of my sweats to keep myself at a matter- of- fact phase. They sounded to belong to another age, an aged age, an age when effects spiritual were different from this of ours, lower certain; an age when foreshadowing's and witches were believable, and ghosts beyond denying. Their very actuality was spectral; the cut of their apparel, fashions born in dead smarts. The beautifiers and conveniences of the room about them were ghostly-- the studies of dissolved men, which still visited rather than shared in the world of to- day. But with an trouble I transferred similar studies to the right- about. The long, draughty subsurface passage was chilly and fine, and my candle burned and made the murk grovel and quake. The echoes chimed up and down the helical staircase, a shadow came sweeping up after me, and one fled before me into the darkness outflow. I came to the wharf and stopped there for a moment, harkening to a rustling that I fancied I heard; also, satisfied of the absolute silence, I pushed open the baize- covered door and stood in the corridor.

The effect was scarcely what I anticipated, for the moonlight, coming in by the great window on the grand staircase, picked out everything in pictorial black shadow or argentine illumination. Everything was in its place the house might have been deserted on the history rather of eighteen months agone. There were candles in the sockets of the sconces, and whatever dust had gathered on the carpets or upon the polished flooring was distributed so unevenly as to be unnoticeable in the moonlight. I was about to advance, and stopped suddenly. A citation group stood upon the wharf, hidden from me by the corner of the wall, but its shadow fell with marvellous otherness upon the white panelling, and gave me the print of someone hunkering to ambuscade me. I stood rigid for half a nanosecond maybe. also, with my hand in the fund that held my revolver, I advanced, only to discover a Ganymede and Eagle glistering in the moonlight. That incident for a time restored my whim-whams, and a demitasse Chinaman on a buhl table, whose head rocked quietly as I passed him, scarcely startled me.

The door to the red room and the way up to it were in a shadowy corner. I moved my candle from side to side, in order to see easily the nature of the recess in which I stood before opening the door. Then it was, allowed I, that my precursor was set up, and the memory of that story gave me a unforeseen pain of apprehension. I glanced over my shoulder at the Ganymede in the moonlight, and opened the door of the red room rather hastily, with my face half turned to the cadaverous silence of the wharf.

I entered, closed the door behind me at formerly, turned the key I set up in the cinch in, and stood with the candle held above, surveying the scene of my surveillance, the great red room of Lorraine Castle, in which the youthful duke had failed. Or, rather, in which he'd begun his dying, for he'd opened the door and fallen headlong down the way I had just mounted. That had been the end of his surveillance, of his gallant attempt to conquer the ghostly tradition of the place, and noway , I allowed, had apoplexy better served the ends of superstition. And there were other and aged stories that cleaved to the room, back to the half-believable morning of it all, the tale of a skittish woman and the woeful end that came to her hubby's jest of shocking her. And looking around that large murky room, with its shadowy window kudos, its recesses and alcoves, one could well understand the legends that had picked in its black corners, its growing darkness. My candle was a little lingo of light in its hugeness, that failed to pierce the contrary end of the room, and left an ocean of riddle and suggestion beyond its islet of light.

I resolved to make a methodical examination of the place at formerly, and disband the fantastic suggestions of its obscurity before they attained a hold upon me. After satisfying myself of the fastening of the door, I began to walk about the room, gaping round each composition of cabinetwork, put away up the valances of the bed, and opening its curtains wide. I pulled up the hangouts and examined the fastenings of the several windows before closing the shutters, leant forward and looked up the blackness of the wide chimney stack, and tapped the dark oak paneling for any secret opening. There were two big glasses in the room, each with a brace of sconces bearing candles, and on the mantelshelf, too, were more candles in demitasse candlesticks. All these I lit one after the other. The fire was laid, an unanticipated consideration from the old char,-- and I lit it, to keep down any disposition to shiver, and when it was burning well, I stood round with my reverse to it and regarded the room again. I had pulled up a chintz- covered arm- president and a table, to form a kind of hedge before me, and on this lay my revolver ready to hand. My precise examination had done me good, but I still set up the closer darkness of the place, and its perfect stillness, too stimulating for the imagination. The echoing of the stir and crackling of the fire was no kind of comfort to me. The shadow in the alcove at the end in particular, had that undefinable quality of a presence, that odd suggestion of a lurking, living thing, that comes so fluently in silence and solitariness. At last, to assure myself, I walked with a candle into it, and satisfied myself that there was nothing palpable there. I stood that candle upon the bottom of the alcove, and left it in that position.

By this time I was in a state of considerable nervous pressure, although to my reason there was no acceptable cause for the condition. My mind, still, was impeccably clear. I supposed relatively unreservedly that nothing supernatural could be, and to pass the time I began to string some rhymes together, Ingoldsby fashion, of the original legend of the place. A many I spoke audibly, but the echoes weren't affable. For the same reason I also abandoned, after a time, a discussion with myself upon the impossibility of ghosts and haunting. My mind regressed to the three old and malformed people downward , and I tried to keep it upon that content. The murky reds and blacks of the room troubled, me; indeed with seven candles the place was simply dim. The bone in the alcove burned in a draught, and the fire- fluttering kept the murk and penumbra constantly shifting and stirring. Casting about for a remedy, I recalled the candles I had seen in the passage, and, with a slight trouble, walked out into the moonlight, carrying a candle and leaving the door open, and presently returned with as numerous as ten. These I put in colorful knick- knacks of demitasse with which the room was sparsely adorned, lit and placed where the murk had lain deepest, some on the bottom, some in the window recesses, until at last my seventeen candles were so arranged that not an inch of the room but had the direct light of at least one of them. It passed to me that when the ghost came, I could advise him not to trip over them. The room was now relatively brightly illuminated. There was commodity veritably cheery and reassuring in these little streaming dears, and smelling them gave me an occupation, and swung a helpful sense of the passage of time. Indeed with that, still, the miscarrying anticipation of the surveillance counted heavily upon me. It was after night that the candle in the alcove suddenly went out, and the black shadow sprang back to its place there. I didn't see the candle go out; I simply turned and saw that the darkness was there, as one might start and see the unanticipated presence of a foreigner." By Jove!" said I audibly;" that draught's a strong bone!" and, taking the matches from the table, I walked across the room in a tardy manner, to relight the corner again. My first match would not strike, and as I succeeded with the alternate, commodity sounded to blink on the wall before me. I turned my head inevitably, and saw that the two candles on the little table by the fireplace were extinguished. I rose at formerly to my bases.

"Odd!" I said." Did I do that myself in a flash of absent- mindedness?"

I walked back, relit one, and as I did so, I saw the candle in the right sconce of one of the glasses wink and go right out, and nearly incontinently its companion followed it. There was no mistake about it. The honey dissolved, as if the wicks had been suddenly nipped between a cutlet and a thumb, leaving the wick neither glowing nor smoking, but black. While I stood peering, the candle at the bottom of the bed went out, and the murk sounded to take another step towards me.

"This will not do!" said I, and first one and also another candle on the mantelshelf followed.

"What is over?" I cried, with a queer high note getting into my voice ever. At that the candle on the wardrobe went out, and the bone I had relit in the alcove followed.

"Steady on!" I said." These candles are wanted," speaking with a half-hysterical flightiness, and scratching down at a match the while for the mantel candlesticks. My hands quivered so important that doubly I missed the rough paper of the matchbox. As the mantel surfaced from darkness again, two candles in the remoter end of the window were transcended. But with the same match I also relit the larger glass candles, and those on the bottom near the doorway, so that for the moment I sounded to gain on the demolitions. But also in a blitz there dissolved four lights at formerly in different corners of the room, and I struck another match in jiggling haste, and stood scrupling whither to take it.

As I stood undecided, an unnoticeable hand sounded to sweep out the two candles on the table. With a cry of terror, I dashed at the alcove, also into the corner, and also into the window, relighting three, as two further dissolved by the fireplace; also, perceiving a better way, I dropped the matches on the iron- bound deed- box in the corner, and caught up the bedroom candlestick. With this I avoided the detention of striking matches; but for all that the steady process of extermination went on, and the murk I stressed and fought against returned, and crept in upon me, first a step gained on this side of me and also on that. It was like a ragged storm- pall sweeping out the stars. Now and also one returned for a nanosecond, and was lost again. I was now nearly frantic with the horror of the coming darkness, and my tone- possession deserted me. I bounded panting and confused from candle to candle, in a vain struggle against that shameless advance.

I bruised myself on the ham against the table, I transferred a president headlong, I stumbled and fell and whisked the cloth from the table in my fall. My candle rolled down from me, and I snared another as I rose. Suddenly this was blown out, as I swung it off the table by the wind of my unforeseen movement, and incontinently the two remaining candles followed. But there was light still in the room, a red light that staved off the murk from me. The fire! Of course, I could still thrust my candle between the bars and relight it!

I turned to where the dears were still dancing between the glowing coals, and splashing red reflections upon the cabinetwork, made two way towards the grate, and directly the dears downscaled and dissolved, the gleam dissolved, the reflections rushed together and dissolved, and as I thrust the candle between the bars darkness closed upon me like the shutting of an eye, wrapped about me in a stifling grasp, sealed my vision, and crushed the last vestiges of reason from my brain. The candle fell from my hand. I slung out my arms in a vain trouble to thrust that ponderous blackness down from me, and, lifting up my voice, screamed with all my might-- formerly, doubly, thrice. also I suppose I must have staggered to my bases. I know I allowed suddenly of the moonlit corridor, and, with my head bowed and my arms over my face, made a run for the door.

But I had forgotten the exact position of the door, and struck myself heavily against the corner of the bed. I staggered back, turned, and was either struck or struck myself against some other big cabinetwork. I've a vague memory of shelling myself therefore, to and down in the darkness, of a confined struggle, and of my own wild weeping as I danced to and down, of a heavy blow at last upon my forepart, a horrible sensation of falling that lasted an age, of my last frantic trouble to keep my footing, and also I flash back no further.

I opened my eyes in daylight. My head was roughly swathed, and the man with the withered arm was watching my face. I looked about me, trying to flash back what had happed, and for a space I couldn't recollect. I rolled my eyes into the corner, and saw the old woman, no longer absentminded, pouring out some drops of drug from a little blue phial into a glass." Where am I?" I asked;" I feel to flash back you, and yet I can not flash back who you are."

They told me also, and I heard of the haunted Red Room as one who hears a tale." We set up you at dawn," said he," and there was blood on your forepart and lips."

It was veritably sluggishly I recovered my memory of my experience." You believe now," said the old man," that the room is visited?" He spoke no longer as one who greets an meddler, but as one who grieves for a broken friend.

"Yes," said I;" the room is visited."

"And you have seen it. And we, who have lived then all our lives, have noway set eyes upon it. Because we've noway dared. Tell us, is it truly the old earl who----"

"No," said I;" it is not."

"I told you so," said the old lady, with the glass in her hand." It's his poor youthful duchess who was alarmed----"

"It's not," I said." There's neither ghost of earl nor ghost of duchess in that room, there's no ghost there at all; but worse, far worse----"

"Well?" they said.

"The worst of all the effects that hang poor mortal man," said I;" and that is, in all its bareness-- Fear that won't have light nor sound, that won't bear with reason, that deafens and darkens and overwhelms. It followed me through the corridor, it fought against me in the room----" I stopped suddenly. There was an interval of silence. My hand went up to my tapes.

Also the man with the shade soughed and spoke." That's it," said he." I knew that was it. A power of darkness. To put such a curse upon a woman! It lurks there always. You can feel it indeed in the day, indeed of a bright summer's day, in the declensions, in the curtains, keeping behind you still you face about. In the dusk it creeps along the corridor and follows you, so that you dare not turn. There's Fear in that room of hers-- black Fear, and there will be-- so long as this house of sin endures."

Chapter No 2: The Terrible Old Man

It was the design of Angelo Ricci and Joe Czanek and Manuel Silva to call on the Terrible Old Man. This old man dwells each alone in a veritably ancient house on Water Street near the ocean, and is reputed to be both exceedingly rich and exceedingly delicate; which forms a situation veritably seductive to men of the profession of Messrs. Ricci, Czanek, and Silva, for that profession was nothing lower staid than thievery.

The occupants of Kingsport say and suppose numerous effects about the Terrible Old Man which generally keep him safe from the attention of gentlemen like Mr. Ricci and his associates, despite the nearly certain fact that he hides a fortune of indefinite magnitude nearly about his musty and venerable residence. He is, in verity, a veritably strange person, believed to have been a captain of East India clipper vessels in his day; so old that no bone can flash back when he was youthful, and so dumb that many know his real name. Among the gnarled trees in the front yard of his aged and neglected place he maintains a strange collection of large monuments, oddly grouped and painted so that they act the icons in some obscure Eastern tabernacle. This collection frightens down utmost of the small boys who love to tease the Terrible Old Man about his long white hair and beard, or to break the small- paned windows of his dwelling with wicked dumdums; but there are other effects which scarify the aged and further curious folk who occasionally steal up to the house to peer in through the fine panes. These folk say that on a table in a bare room on the ground bottom are numerous peculiar bottles, in each a small piece of lead suspended pendulum-wise from a string. And they say that the Terrible Old Man talks to these bottles, addressing them by similar names as Jack, Scar- Face, Long Tom, Spanish Joe, Peters, and Mate Ellis, and that whenever he speaks to a bottle the little lead pendulum within makes certain definite climate as if in answer.

Those who have watched the altitudinous, spare, Terrible Old Man in these peculiar exchanges, don't watch him again. But Angelo Ricci and Joe Czanek and Manuel Silva weren't of Kingsport blood; they were of that new and miscellaneous alien stock which lies outside the entranced circle of New England life and traditions, and they saw in the Terrible Old Man simply a tottering, nearly helpless slate- beard, who couldn't walk without the aid of his interlaced club, and whose thin, weak hands shook pitifully. They were really relatively sorry in their way for the lonely, unpopular old fellow, whom everybody escaped, and at whom all the tykes barked singularly. But business is business, and to a purloiner whose soul is in his profession, there's a lure and a challenge about a veritably old and veritably delicate man who has no account at the bank, and who pays for his many musts at the vill store with Spanish gold and tableware formed two centuries agone.

Ricci, Czanek, and Silva named the night of April 11 for their call. Mr. Ricci and Mr. Silva were to solicit the poor old gentleman, whilst Mr. Czanek awaited for them and their presumable metallic burden with a covered motor- auto in Ship Street, by the gate in the altitudinous hinder wall of their hosts grounds. Desire to avoid dispensable explanations in case of unanticipated police intrusions urged these plans for a quiet and unostentatious departure.

As prearranged, the three comers started out independently in order to help any wrong-inclined reservations subsequently. Messrs. Ricci and Silva met in Water Street by the old man's frontal gate, and although they didn't like the way the moon shone down upon the painted monuments through the budding branches of the gnarled trees, they had more important effects to suppose about than bare idle superstition. They stressed it might be unwelcome work making the Terrible Old Man garrulous concerning his hoarded gold and tableware, for aged ocean- captains are specially stubborn and perverse. Still, he was veritably old and veritably delicate, and there were two callers. Messrs. Ricci and Silva were endured in the art of making unintentional persons voluble, and the riots of a weak and exceptionally venerable man can be fluently muffled. So they moved up to the one lighted window and heard the Terrible Old Man talking childishly to his bottles with pendulums. also they slipped masks and knocked politely at the rainfall- stained oaken door.

Staying sounded veritably long to Mr. Czanek as he tossed restlessly in the covered motor- auto by the Terrible Old Man's aft gate in Ship Street. He was further than naturally tender- hearted, and he didn't like the hideous riots he'd heard in the ancient house just after the hour appointed for the deed. Had he not told his associates to be as gentle as possible with the pathetic old ocean- captain? veritably nervously he watched that narrow oaken gate in the high and ivy- sheathe gravestone wall. constantly he consulted his watch, and wondered at the detention. Had the old man failed before revealing where his treasure was hidden, and had a thorough hunt come necessary? Mr. Czanek didn't like to stay so long in the dark in such a place. also he tasted a soft tread or tapping on the walk inside the gate, heard a gentle fumbling at the gravel latch, and saw the narrow, heavy door swing inward. And in the cadaverous gleam of the single dim road- beacon he strained his eyes to see what his associates had brought out of that minatory house which impended so near before. But when he looked, he didn't see what he'd anticipated; for his associates weren't there at each, but only the Terrible Old Man leaning still on his interlaced club and smiling hideously. Mr. Czanek had noway before noticed the color of that mans eyes; now he saw that they were unheroic.

Little Effects make considerable excitement in little municipalities, which is the reason that Kingsport people talked all that spring and summer about the three unidentifiable bodies, horribly slashed as with numerous scimitars, and horribly mangled as by the tread of numerous cruel charge- heels, which the drift washed in. And some people indeed spoke of effects as trivial as the vacated motor- auto set up in Ship Street, or certain especially inhuman cries, presumably of a slapdash beast or migrant raspberry, heard in the night by awake citizens. But in this idle vill gossip the Terrible Old Man took no interest at all. He was by nature reserved, and when one is aged and delicate, one's reserve is twice strong. Either, so ancient an ocean- captain must have witnessed scores of effects much more stirring in the far-off days of his unremembered youth.

Chapter No 3: A Ghost Story

I took a large room, far up Broadway, in a huge old structure whose upper stories had been wholly unoccupied for times until I came. The place had long been given up to dust and cobwebs, to solitariness and silence. I sounded feeling among the sepultures and overrunning the sequestration of the dead, that first night I climbed up to my diggings. For the first time in my life a superstitious dread came over me; and as I turned a dark angle of the stairway and an unnoticeable cobweb swung its slazy woof in my face and clung there, I jounced as one who had encountered a phantom.

I was glad enough when I reached my room and locked out the earth and the darkness. A cheery fire was burning in the grate, and I sat down before it with a comforting sense of relief. For two hours I sat there, thinking of defunct times; recalling old scenes, and summoning half- forgotten faces out of the mists of the history; listening, in fancy, to voices that long agone grew silent for all time, and to formerly familiar songs that nothing sings now. And as my study softened down to a sadder and sadder pathos, the shrieking of the winds outside softened to a wail, the angry beating of the rain against the panes lowered to a tranquil jargon, and one by one the noises in the road subsided, until the whisking steps of the last delinquent crawler failed down in the distance and left no sound behind.

The fire had burned low. A sense of loneliness crept over me. I arose and undressed, moving on slide about the room, doing stealthily what I had to do, as if I were encircled by sleeping adversaries whose slumbers it would be fatal to break. I covered up in bed, and lay harkening to the rain and wind and the faint creaking of distant shutters, till they tranquilized me to sleep.

I slept profoundly, but how long I don't know. All at formerly I set up myself awake, and filled with a jouncing expectation. All was still. All but my own heart-- I could hear it beat. Presently the bedclothes began to slip down sluggishly toward the bottom of the bed, as if some one were pulling them! I couldn't stir; I couldn't speak. Still the robes slipped designedly down, till my bone was uncovered. also with a great trouble I seized them and drew them over my head. I awaited, heeded, awaited. Once further that steady pull began, and formerly more I lay torpid a century of dragging seconds till my bone was naked again. At last I roused my powers and snared the covers back to their place and held them with a strong grip. I awaited. By and by I felt a faint haul, and took a fresh grip. The haul strengthened to a steady strain-- it grew stronger and stronger. My hold parted, and for the third time the robes slid down. I moaned. An answering moan came from the bottom of the bed! Rounded drops of sweat stood upon my forepart. I was more dead than alive. Presently I heard a heavy step in my room-- the step of an giant, it sounded to me-- it wasn't like anything mortal. But it was moving from me-- there was relief in that. I heard it approach the door-- pass out without moving bolt or cinch-- and wander away among the dismal corridors, straining the bottoms and joists till they creaked again as it passed-- and also silence reigned formerly more.

When my excitement had calmed, I said to myself," This is a dream-- simply a hideous dream." And so I lay allowing it over until I induced myself that it was a dream, and also a comforting laugh relaxed my lips and I was happy again. I got up and struck a light; and when I set up that the cinches and bolts were just as I had left them, another soothing laugh welled in my heart and gurgled from my lips. I took my pipe and lit it, and was just sitting down before the fire, when- down went the pipe out of my nerveless fritters, the blood quit my cheeks, and my placid breathing was cut short with a rustle! In the ashes on the domicile, side by side with my own bare footmark, was another, so vast that in comparison mine was but an child's! also I had had a caller, and the giant tread was explained.

I put out the light and returned to bed, palsied with fear. I lay a long time, gaping into the darkness, and harkening. -- also I heard a grating noise above, like the dragging of a heavy body across the bottom; also the throwing down of the body, and the shaking of my windows in response to the concussion. In distant corridor of the structure I heard the muffled slamming of doors. I heard, at intervals, stealthy steps creeping in and out among the corridors, and over and down the stairs. occasionally these noises approached my door, dithered, and went down again. I heard the clopping of chains noiselessly, in remote passages, and heeded while the clopping grew nearer-- while it wearily climbed the stairways, marking each move by the loose fat of chain that fell with an featured rattle upon each succeeding step as the troll that bore it advanced. I heard murmured rulings; half-uttered riots that sounded smothered violently; and the swish of unnoticeable garments, the rush of unnoticeable bodies. also I came conscious that my chamber was raided-- that I wasn't alone. I heard sighs and breathings about my bed, and mysterious whisperings. Three little spheres of soft phosphorescent light appeared on the ceiling directly over my head, clung and glowed there a moment, and also dropped-- two of them upon my face and one upon the pillow. They, spattered, liquidly, and felt warm. Suspicion told me they had-- turned to gouts of blood as they fell-- I demanded no light to satisfy myself of that. also I saw cadaverous faces, dimly luminous, and white upraised hands, floating formless in the air-- floating a moment and also fading. The rumbling desisted, and the voices and the sounds, anal a solemn stillness followed. I awaited and heeded. I felt that I must have light or die. I was weak with fear. I sluggishly raised myself toward a sitting posture, and my face came in contact with a glacial hand! All strength went from me supposedly, and I fell back like a stricken invalid. Also I heard the howl of a garment it sounded to pass to the door and go out.

When everything was still formerly more, I crept out of bed, sick and delicate, and lit the gas with a hand that quivered as if it were progressed with a hundred times. The light brought some little cheer to my spirits. I sat down and fell into a comforting contemplation of that great footmark in the ashes. By and by its outlines began to waver and grow dim. I glanced up and the broad gas- honey was sluggishly wilting down. In the same moment I heard that elephantine tread again. I noted its approach, nearer and nearer, along the musty halls, and dimmer and dimmer the light waned. The tread reached my very door and broke-- the light had downscaled to a sickly blue, and all effects about me lay in a spectral twilight. The door didn't open, and yet I felt a faint gust of air addict my impertinence, and presently was conscious of a huge, cloudy presence before me. I watched it with fascinated eyes. A pale gleam stole over the Thing; gradationally its cloudy crowds took shape an arm appeared, also legs, also a body, and last a great sad face looked out of the vapor. Stripped of its filmy jackets, naked, muscular and comely, the majestic Cardiff Giant impended above me!

All my misery dissolved-- for a child might know that no detriment could come with that benignant countenance. My cheerful spirits returned at formerly, and in sympathy with them the gas flamed up brightly again. noway a lonely castaway was so glad to drink company as I was to hail the friendly mammoth. I said

"Why, is it nothing but you? Do you know, I've been spooked to death for the last two or three hours? I'm most actually glad to see you. I wish I had a president-- Then, then, do not try to sit down in that thing--"

But it was too late. He was in it before I could stop him and down he went-- I noway saw a president fiddled so in my life.

"Stop, stop, you will ruin eve--"

Too late again. There was another crash, and another president was resolved into its original rudiments.

"Confound it, have not you got any judgment at' all? Do you want to ruin all the cabinetwork on the place? Then, then, you petrified fool--"

But it was no use. Before I could arrest him he'd sat down on the bed, and it was a melancholy ruin.

"Now what kind of a way is that to do? First you come lumbering about the place bringing a legion of vagabond leprechauns along with you to worry me to death, and also when I overlook an vulgarity of costume which would not be permitted anywhere by cultivated people except in a respectable theater, and not indeed there if the bareness were of your coitus, you repay me by stranding all the cabinetwork you can find to sit down on. And why will you? You damage yourself as much as you do me. You have broken off the end of your spinal column, and littered up the bottom with chips of your hams till the place looks like a marble yard. You ought to be ashamed of yourself-- you are big enough to know more."

"Well, I'll not break any further cabinetwork. But what am I to do? I haven't had a chance to sit down for a century." And the gashes came into his eyes.

"Poor devil," I said," I shouldn't have been so harsh with you. And you're an orphan, too, no mistrustfulness. But sit down on the bottom then-- nothing differently can stand your weight-- and besides, we can not be sociable with you down over there above me; I want you down where I can perch on this high counting- house coprolite and gossip with you face to face." So he sat down on the bottom, and lit a pipe which I gave him, threw one of my red robes over his shoulders, reversed my sitz- bath on his head, helmet fashion, and made himself graphic and comfortable. also he crossed his ankles, while I renewed the fire, and exposed the flat, honeycombed bottoms of his fabulous bases to the thankful warmth.

"What's the matter with the bottom of your bases and the reverse of your legs, that they're overcharged up so?"

"Freaking chilblains-- I caught them clear up to the reverse of my head, roosting out there under Newell's ranch. But I love the place; I love it as one loves his old home. There's no peace for me like the peace I feel when I'm there."

We talked along for half an hour, and also I noticed that he looked tired, and spoke of it.

"Tired?" he said." Well, I should suppose so. And now I'll tell you all about it, since you have treated me so well. I'm the spirit of the Petrified Man that lies across the road there in the gallery. I'm the ghost of the Cardiff Giant. I can have no rest, no peace, till they've given that poor body burial again. Now what was the most natural thing for me to do, to make men satisfy this want? scarify them into it! hang the place where the body lay! So I visited the gallery night after night. I indeed got other spirits to help me. But it did no good, for nothing ever came to the gallery at night. also it passed to me to come over the way and hang this place a little. I felt that if I ever got a hail I must succeed, for I had the most effective company that Tophet could furnish. Night after night we've fiddled around through these mildewed halls, dragging chains, moaning, bruiting , tramping up and down stairs, till, to tell you the verity, I'm nearly worn out. But when I saw a light in your room to-night I roused my powers again and went at it with a deal of the old newness. But I'm tired out-- entirely wearied out. Give me, I solicit you, give me some hope!" I lit off my perch in a burst of excitement, and blatted

"This transcends everything! everything that ever did do! Why you poor blundering old reactionary, you have had all your trouble for nothing-- you have been hanging a cataplasm cast of yourself-- the real Cardiff Giant is in Albany!--(A fact. The original fraud was ingeniously and fraud fully duplicated, and displayed in New York as the" only genuine" Cardiff Giant(to the inenarrable nausea of the possessors of the real giant) at the veritably same time that the ultimate was drawing crowds at a gallery is Albany,)-- Confound it, do not you know your own remains?"

I noway saw such an eloquent look of shame, of pitiable demotion, overspread a countenance ahead.

The Petrified Man rose sluggishly to his bases, and said

"Actually, is that true?"

"As true as I'm sitting then."

He took the pipe from his mouth and laid it on the mantel, also stood irresolute a moment (unconsciously, from old habit, thrusting his hands where his pantaloons pockets should have been, and meditatively dropping his chin on his bone); and eventually said

"Well- I noway felt so absurd before. The Petrified Man has vended everybody differently, and now the mean fraud has ended by dealing its own ghost! My son, if there's any charity left in your heart for a poor friendless phantom like me, do not let this get out. Suppose how you would feel if you had made such a burro of yourself."

I heard his stately tramp die down, gradually down the stairs and out into the vacated road, and felt sorry that he was gone, poor fellow-- and sorrier still that he'd carried off my red mask and my bath- hogshead.

Chapter No 4: Don't Think About It

Tommy was not really a skittish child. Occasionally he did not understand effects and was puzzled. More frequently, grown- ups could not or wouldn't understand effects that were impeccably clear to him and he was more puzzled. Sometimes similar effects upset and indeed upset him a little. Also Momma and occasionally Daddy would restate befuddlement into silly adult terms and suppose that he was hysterical.

It was that way about the hole in the closet when Tommy was just a bit over three. Tommy was not really hysterical. Mr. Bear was hysterical and the thing did mystification Tommy. So he asked about it, but he noway did get any sensible or satisfactory answers, and that did worry and maybe indeed upset him a little.

But he was not hysterical, indeed before Daddy eventually told him," Now, Tommy, boy. Do not suppose about it and it will not scarify you. Really, there is nothing there to hurt you, if you just do not suppose about it. So do not you suppose about it any more — there's Daddy's big boy."

This clearly wasn't any kind of explanation. But still Tommy did try hard not to suppose about it, as Daddy said. And now he really does not suppose about it at all any more. Or about Aunt Martha, moreover.

The hole was in the closet in Tommy's room. Tommy and Momma and Daddy lived in a not veritably big, not veritably new frame house on the edge of the megacity and Aunt Martha lived with them. Tommy didn't — at least not yet, although there were pledges have any sisters or sisters. But he did have his own room and a family of his own, too. It was the redundant bedroom and it had a closet that was confined and with no light. Tommy liked his room. It was small, with a small bed, and it belonged to him, along with his family of Mr. Bear and Old Rabbit and Kokey Koala. It was also in easy crying range of Momma and Daddy's room and Aunt Martha's room, so if Mr. Bear, who was the skittish one, got frighted in the night, Tommy could cry — purely in Mr. Bear's behalf — to bring help. Or at least company.

Tommy and his family all liked the closet well enough too, except for the shelf that was out of reach indeed from the" don't climb" coprolite. The closet was good to hide in or play bear delve or rabbit hole and forfeiture for chancing missing toys after Momma had a spell of playing drawing house.

The day Tommy set up the hole in the closet was the week after his third birthday. Daddy was at work. Mammy was out shopping. It was a stormy autumn. Aunt Martha was sitting with Tommy and the autumn TV.

He was in his room with his family and they all agreed as soon as they heard the TV coming on strong that it would be a veritably poor autumn to waste on a nap. Either, Mr. Bear's passions had been hurt by having been kindly left out of effects lately in favor of new birthday presents, now largely broken or tiresome. To make it up to him, Tommy and Old Rabbit and Kokey each agreed to play bear delve in the closet. It was a nice game and going well enough, except for some growling from Kokey Koala, who always wanted to argue and claimed that bears lived in trees, not grottoes .

But also — and it was Mr. Bear's fault for wanting it darker, so he could hibernate — the closet door shut tight. That did not feel so serious at first. It would only mean a scolding for being out of bed when Aunt Martha would come to open it after Tommy cried loud enough. And also there was the hole in the closet, back in the corner next to the broken barrel. They all saw it and they heard the Ugly Thing talking or allowing at them. It stretched out a part of itself at Mr. Bear, who was the closest.

It did not snare Mr. Bear, but he was scarified just the same. And none of them liked it. They did not like it at all. The Ugly Thing could not come out of the hole because the hole was not big enough yet, but it tried and it was making the hole bigger. And it kept allowing at them, red studies, and empty, as it tore at the edges of the hole. The family all looked to Tommy, so Tommy cried and yelled.

Eventually Aunt Martha heard him and came to open the door. also the autumn sun streamed across the bottom into the closet and the unattractive red studies from the Thing pulled back, far back, so you could slightly notice them, and you could not see the hole any more, indeed though you knew it was still there. At least Tommy and Mr. Bear and Old Rabbit and Kokey Koala knew.

After she opened the closet door and carried Tommy from the closet to the living room, Aunt Martha scolded. She was not really frenetic because she had awaited until a marketable intruded her TV program before answering the cries from the closet. But she scolded because she was Aunt Martha and scolding was what Aunt Martha did. A really good cry, indeed one worked up rigorously as a service for a companion, takes a little time to turn off. also, after a many settling drafts, Tommy tried to explain.

"Auntie. Aunt Martha, there is a hole in the delve

— in the closet — and there is a Thing inside of it."

He looked at Mr. Bear whom he was holding by one bottom and at Kokey, dropped by Aunt Martha on the lounge, for evidence. also, snappily, he wriggled down from Auntie's stage. Old Rabbit!

Bravely, Tommy ran to the closet and was relieved. The door was open and, in the argentine autumn light, the hole was still not to be seen. Old Rabbit, who always had a bad temper, was irked and pettish at having been left before. But he was there and each right. Tommy saved him and ran back to Aunt Martha.

"It was empty," he continued his explanation.

Aunt Martha, as always, was delicate." Who's empty? You should not be empty, Tommy. You just had your lunch an hour agone

. Do you want a glass of milk?"

"Not me empty." Tommy was intolerant. Aunt Martha noway sounded suitable to grasp any idea more complex than a glass of milk or wet pants. Little boys, in her mind, nearly always either wanted the one or had the other. similar effects she could and did attend to with a righteous sense of duty done. But anything differently was beyond her.

"Tommy! Are your pants wet?"

Tommy soughed in abdication and wet his pants. It was the only thing to do. else Auntie would fuss and cloud, negotiating nothing, understanding nothing, for the rest of the autumn.

Ten twinkles latterly, in dry pants, he finished an unwanted glass of milk. Aunt Martha, heart gentled, returned to cleaner pieces. Tommy and his family, nap safely forgotten, played down the autumn but not in the closet or indeed, as was usual on stormy days, in Tommy's room. Rather, chancing Daddy's old briefcase full of papers, they played office in the family room, with Old Rabbit growling about having to be Miss Wicksey, who drove the electric typewriter in Daddy's office.

Mammy and Daddy came home together at a bit after five. Tommy took his scolding about intruding up Daddy's papers in good part. He'd anticipated it. But Aunt Martha was angry about the scolding she got for letting him, mild though it was.

In retribution, she said," Tommy, you were a mischievous, mischievous boy. And for being so mischievous you must take your big bear and your rabbit and the little bear or whatever the thing is and put them down in the closet. And leave them there till hereafter."

"No! No, no, no, I will not! It is not fair. They were not bad. And the Ugly Thing is in the hole and it might come out and it's empty and — and my family is each hysterical."

"Tommy!" Aunt Martha's voice was sharp." You stop that gibberish and put your toys"

"Stay. Stay up now," said Daddy, who also lived in the grown- up world, but who occasionally, tried to understand effects." What is this about a hole in the closet? What about commodity being empty?"

"That is all," said Tommy." The Ugly Thing in the hole in the closet. It's empty."

There was further to it than that, of course, but how could a thing like that be explained through a wall of grown, closed minds? There was the hole in the closet. You could not exactly see it. You could only sort of feel seeing it and the hairy Thing — at least it sounded hairy and shapeless, or having numerous different shapes and a mouth and sharp teeth — and it had reached out with commodity and touchedMr. Bear and would have eaten him too, if he'd blood. But also it had pulled back fromMr. Bear and red hunger studies came stronger and stronger. Indeed now, stretching out from the hole where it was hidden there in the closet, Tommy could feel the reaching, greedy studies. But he could not explain all that.

" There's a hole in the closet," Tommy said again.

But he knew that not indeed Daddy would understand. Of course Momma wouldn't. Not Momma, who was loving but veritably busy and just sat so frequently, featuring or harkening to baby family that they said was in her stomach, so big and fat now as to leave little stage room. mammy was too engaged looking inward to look out much at Tommy. Daddy, to give him credit, was nearly always willing to look, but there were so numerous effects he could not see. Still Tommy had to try.

"The Ugly Thing in the hole. It wants commodity to eat."

"Oh, Tommy! similar horrible gibberish!" That was Momma. She was not indeed going to suppose about it. It's a question occasionally whether baby sisters are worth all the bother and trouble.

"Now, Tommy." Daddy was being helpful." You say there's a hole in your closet? And that there's commodity in the hole?"

"Well- ll. kind of." Really, the Ugly Thing was not so important in the hole as on the other side of it. But that was close enough.

"Each right also, Tommy. Suppose you show it to me."

"What?"

"Show me the hole, Tommy."

"Now?"

"Yes."

"The hole in the closet?"

"Tommy!"

"Yes, Daddy." This was not going to work out to anything good and Tommy did not want to go back to the closet and close the closet door anyway. The Thing did not eat Mr. Bear because Mr. Bear did not have blood. But Daddy had and." Tommy!"

They went to the closet. At least, if he was risking a Daddy, Tommy allowed

, he was guarding Mr. Bear and the others.

"Now where is this hole, Tommy?"

"Over there by the corner." Tommy refocused.

Daddy went into the closet to look. Tommy started to close the door. In the black dark, Daddy would see what Tommy meant about the Thing in the hole. From the outside, Tommy started to close the door. It was a small closet and hardly big enough for both of them.

"Tommy! What are you trying to do? Open that door."

"But" After all, the hole was not there, or scarcely sounded to be there, except in the dark.

"Open it up wider. Hm-m. I believe I do see. stay till I get my lighter. Say, by George, I believe you are right. There's a little hole there. Looks like a mouse hole."

There it was, as Tommy might have known. Overgrown- ups will always avoid seeing the important effects. Of course there was a mouse hole there, the home of the little old Mr. Mouse with the wriggly nose and the argentine whiskers. He'd been nice. But he was not there any more and Tommy had a enough clear idea of what had happed to him. That poor little old Mr. Mouse had had blood.

"But, Daddy —"

It was hopeless." Dorrie! Martha!" Daddy's stalking instinct was aroused." Have we got a mouse trap? Any rubbish? There's a hole in that closet, a little old mouse hole and I am going to —"

Well, maybe this would be better than if he had not set up anything.

Tommy followed Daddy about as he eventually located a mouse trap. No rubbish? He cut a little piece of meat for bait. Of course Tommy knew no trap would catch the Ugly Thing.

"What in the world happed to my lighter?" Daddy wanted to know. Tommy did not answer that. But at least everybody, indeed Aunt Martha, had forgotten about shutting Tommy's family up in the closet. For now that was enough.

But latterly, after supper, after bath, after the firing picture on the television, it was time for bed.

"Daddy?"

"Get on to bed now, son. once bedtime. Hop to it."

"Daddy, I want to sleep with you and Momma tonight."

Well, it was a potent dark night. The autumn rain had erected up into a real storm. Mr. Bear was alarmed. Kokey was spooked and indeed tough Old Rabbit did not want to sleep in Tommy's room with the Ugly Thing in the hole so empty and staying to rip its way out of the hole when it got dark enough — and only the road light outside the room to keep down the dark because they would noway let Tommy keep his light on at night.

"My family and me do not want to sleep in my room tonight."

"Now, Tommy, just because it's a little stormy — Daddy's big boy is not hysterical of a little wind and rain?"

"I am not hysterical , Daddy. It's my family. You know how families are. You always say about Momma"

"Noway mind that now. To bed. Your own bed."

"But Daddy, there is the Ugly Thing in the hole! And it's empty!"

"The mouse?"

Daddy went to look at his trap, switching on the light in Tommy's room. He came back in a nanosecond.

"The little devil!"

Did Daddy know? No.

"The little devil got down with the bait, clean as a whoosh. Only a little cataplasm dust or commodity left in the trap where I put the meat."

Bear fiddled." Now do not be foolish, Bear. You do not have blood. The Ugly Thing will not get you," Tommy told him vocally. But Mr. Bear wouldn't hear. He was a cry- baby, a scaredy- cat. But to tell the verity — the real, honest verity — the whole family and indeed Tommy did not feel too good about it.

"Tommy? What was that you were saying?"

"Daddy! I wan na sleep with you and Momma. My family and me. We are spooked of that Thing." Tommy knew it was no lower than his duty to cover them all.

"Oh, now, Tommy! You do not mean to say you are hysterical of a little old mouse? A big boy like you?"

"Well, Mr. Bear is I don't — Daddy! It's there, honest it is, in that hole and it's empty and it will come out in the dark and —"

"Tommy! A little mouse! Get on into your room now and no more argument."

Tommy's face began to crumple. However, he'd fight this one out all the way — gashes, hissy

, If he'd to." Now, now, Tommy- boy." Daddy did mean well and occasionally he was indeed right and so Tommy always did try to do what Daddy said." Tommy, you must not let effects like that bother you. However, forget it, If we can not catch the little mouse. There is nothing further we can do, so just do not suppose about it. You see?"

Sniff." No."

"Do not suppose about it, that is all. There's nothing there that can hurt you, if you just do not suppose about it. So do not suppose about it — that's Daddy's big boy."

"Well- ll. And also can we sleep with you and Momma?"

Aunt Martha chimed in her nickel's worth." A boy ought to be shamed to be hysterical of a little mouse."

"It's not —"

"Not what?"

"Uh it's Mr. Bear that is hysterical . Of the —"

"And you just stop that gibberish about those ridiculous stuffed creatures, you hear me? Nothing should make such a fuss about a little mouse."

"Momma does. mammy!" Tommy let two fat gashes trickle down his cheeks, a warning, but he meant them too." mammy-a-a, can not we —"

"Each right, each right! Stop this stupid wrangling! You know how it gets on my jitters. For virtuousness' sake, let him sleep with us tonight. Anyway, I do not condemn him. I wouldn't sleep a wink in the same room with a mouse. Be sure you shut our door tonight. Tight."

"You are spoiling the child," said Aunt Martha sourly.

"Auntie," said Tommy," I go you are funk to let your door stay open."

"Well!" raved Aunt Martha." The impertinence! I clearly shall keep my door open. No mouse is going to keep me from getting good, fresh air."

Tommy was a veritably bright little boy. Now, with the door shut in Momma and Daddy's room, and Aunt Martha's door open, he wouldn't suppose about the Ugly Thing in the hole — staying for dark, real dark — to come out — and eat.

"Each right, Tommy. This formerly you can sleep with your mama and me. Get on to bed and mind you sleep quiet. And do not spread those stuff — your family each over the bed moreover."

"Yes, Daddy. And, Daddy —"

"What?"

"I will not suppose about it now, the Thing in the hole."

Tommy said his good nights. Tonight he indeed kissed Aunt Martha as if he meant it. And he took his family and he went to bed in Momma and Daddy's room.

He didn't suppose about the Ugly Thing. He went right to sleep, lying at the edge of the big, big bed. Tommy, and Old Rabbit, and Kokey Koala, and indeed Mr. Bear went right to sleep.

Outside the wind blew hard and harder and the rain drove down and it was dark. The TV event was bad. Everyone went to bed beforehand. Good night. Lights out.

In Tommy's room it was relatively dark with only the faint, watery shafts of the road light on the corner swimming in through the rain. In the closet there was a shifting, a fumbling, a tearing and the hole in the blackness grew, was forced, bigger, wider, as the Thing pushed and ripped at whatever was barring it from the warm, red, oozing food it craved; it must have; it would have.

And, in a unforeseen gust, the wind blew harder still. nearly in city, blocks down, a line fell and blue sparks flashed and crepitated in the sopping night. In Tommy's house the refrigerator went off, the electric timepieces stopped. The road light blinked formerly and was gone and in Tommy's closet there was a unforeseen, potent swell of trouble, a break, and commodity, not a sound, but commodity, a harsh and bloody sense or sense of ripping rapacity flowing outward from the closet in a surge.

Aunt Martha, in her sleep, said," No. Oh, no!"

Daddy intruded a snuffle with a simulated grunt. mammy puled vocally and hugged to herself her blown stomach.

Tommy blinked and was awake. Soothingly, he gentled Kokey and Old Rabbit. He squeezed Mr. Bear's paw. also he slipped his hand into the opening in Mr. Bear's overalls and took out Daddy's cigarette lighter. He knew how to work it. But first he awaited.

"Do not suppose about it," Daddy had told him and he did not suppose about it, really. But he could not help feeling it. The Ugly Thing was out, clear out of the hole now, and moving. He could feel that and the awful hunger moving with it. Aunt Martha's room was closest and her door was open. mammy and Daddy's room was closed. The Ugly Thing moved presto, briskly, and reached out, thirsting, hungering.

From Aunt Martha's room came the warbling wail and from the Thing there flowed a sense of vicious, evil joy.

There it was, but was it enough?

Tommy hugged Mr. Bear formerly, tightly, and slipped distinctly from the bed. He was not allowing about it, he couldn't, he wouldn't suppose about it. But he knew what he'd to do. He'd the lighter. At the bedroom door he worked it. Opened the door a crack; thrust it out. And also, in a little rush, back to bed where he lay still, and he did not suppose about it, he and Mr. Bear and Old Rabbit and Kokey Koala.

After a little, the sense of feeding hunger was gone and the sense of the Ugly Thing was gone, back into the hole in the closet, forced back by the fluttering unheroic light of the dears started by the cigarette lighter. also, when the smell of bank grew thick in the room and he could hear the crackling of the fire burning the house, Tommy shook Daddy awake.

It was not hard to get out through the bedroom window, except for Momma. But she made it each right. And Tommy had a little trouble holding tightly to each member of his family as Daddy lifted him out of the window, but they made it each right too. Of course Aunt Martha did not make it — how could she? But it was delightful watching the firemen in the rain from the Krausmeyer's veranda coming door as the house and the closet with the hole in the closet all burned up together.

Aunt Martha?

" Funny thing," Tommy heard one fireman say to another the coming day, in the sun, as they looked over the smouldering ash," the old club must have been as dry as dust outside. Twenty times in the department and I noway did see a body so fully consumed — teeth, a little bone. Hey, get on down from then, son! Get along on home with you!"

Daddy and mammy said Aunt Martha had gone down on a trip. Tommy might have known enough well where she had gone, if he'd allowed about it, but he did not suppose about it. None of his family did. What for? Aunt Martha had had to go down, sure. She went. each right, who missed Aunt Martha?

Anyway, there were lights in all of the closets in the new house they moved to and lots of room for everyone, indeed baby family. And there were no holes, not indeed mouse holes, in any of the closets.

Chapter No 5: The Long Arm

I had been out of Germany for thirty- five times, drawn hither and thither by colorful spangling of will- of- the- wisps. When I returned to my native country, I was as poor in fund as when I left, and important poorer in visions.

The Berlin insurance company which I had represented with similar medium success in Switzerland, Austria and Belgium agreed to let me vend for them at home, and by a curious coexistence there was an opening in the antique old Bavarian megacity in which I had been born and bred.

I'll pass over the strangely mingled passions with which I rode in a Twentieth Century road train past the thousand- time-old walls of one of the most curious ancient metropolises in Europe, a city also whose every winding narrow road and sharp- gabled structure had been the companion of my immaturity and nonage. No bone sounded to know me, and I honored no bone. For several days I made no attempt to vend life insurance, but wandered in a dream, the bewildered ghost of my former tone, about the spots which I had known in happier days.

One dull stormy autumn I took retreat from the rainfall in a dingy little coffee- house in which, at the age of fourteen or fifteen, I on with certain boon companions, had learned the gentle art of billiards. It sounded as if every composition of cabinetwork was just as I had walked down from them, well toward half a century ahead. It was raining outdoors, and I sat alone in the caliginous, hoarse old place, pondering the sweet and bitter mystifications of life.

While I sat therefore, gaping out with unseeing eyes at the rain which was by this time beating down dashingly on the pavement, I came conscious that someone in the room was gaping at me. I hadn't noticed that there was anyone differently in the dark, low- ceilinged place except the obsequious owner who had served me my cigar and coffee. Now I realized that a man who sat in the corner transversely across from me was studying me curiously from over his review. His face was one that I had seen ahead. Suddenly, across all the times, I flashed back him. And in that same moment he rose and came toward me with his hand held out.

We had been in academy together, in the Gymnasium. He'd been a strange fellow with many musketeers, but had enjoyed the character of being the stylish pupil in his class. But in his last time in the Gymnasium he had, for what reason I noway knew, excited the enmity of a dyspeptic old professor who had intimately declared that Gustav wasn't the kind of boy who should have a Gymnasium parchment and that he, the professor, was determined noway to give him a passing grade. My father had respected the boy veritably much, and at one juncture when my marks looked perilously low, he'd employed Gustav to tutor me. Gustav had been so successful that Father was pleased and made him a present of a tableware cigarette case with Gustav's initials and mine engraved on it. I flashed back all this veritably distinctly as we shook hands, but I was doing presto thinking, because for the life of me I could not flash back his strange last name. I had a feeling that it was a veritably foreign name, Polish or Croatian or commodity of the kind. As he mentioned this and that, I sweat I answered him a little absently and incoherently. The name was nearly there. The syllables flirted tantalizingly just out of my reach. But I was sure the name began with aB. Was not it a Bam- or a Ban- commodity? Ah! I had it. Banaotovich!

From that moment the discussion went more fluently. I was surprized and pleased when Banaotovich drew his tableware cigarette- case out of his fund to prove to me how largely he allowed of my poor departed father. We were soon launched on a cordial exchange of nonage recollections. Banaotovich sounded a good- hearted fellow after all, and I wondered why in my nonage I had noway been relatively comfortable in his company. I flashed back that other boys of the group had admitted to me intimately that they were further than a little hysterical of him.

The longer we talked the more intimate, the more in the nature of a collective concession, our discussion came. I admitted to Banaotovich that the hifalutin fashion in which I had left the city to win fame and fortune times ahead, had been asinine in the extreme, and that it served me just right to have to sneak back unknown and poor. Banaotovich replied that for all his pride in his academy marks he'd remained a person of no significance, and that the pot hadn't the fewest intention of making itself ridiculous by calling the kettle dark. He sounded nearly sorrowfully inclined to run himself down. I could feel in his manner a kind of pathetic reaching out for sympathy and consideration. And it began to feel as if he were about to tell me commodity or ask me for commodity. But whatever he'd to tell sounded hard to say, and it was slow in coming over his lips.

Banaotovich ordered two bottles of the heavy native wine. I drank sparingly of it, because it goes to my head. But Banaotovich swallowed two or three glassfuls in hasty race, and his cheeks grew flushed. There was a pause. Suddenly he leaned across the table toward me and spoke in a coarse, agitated tale.

"Modersohn," he said anxiously," I want to make a concession to you — a terrible concession. It may turn you against me fully. perhaps you do not want to hear it. However, say so, and I will go home, If you don't. But it seems as if I have got to tell notoriety about it. It seems as if I have got to find notoriety who understands me and can excuse me, or it'll kill me. Shall I tell you? Shall I?"

I was startled. I was nicely sure that Banaotovich was no miscreant, since he'd lived half a century in his native megacity, unperturbed and from all he'd told me solvent and reputed. I had always known that he was a queer fish, a miscarrying, solitary kind of person, and I settled myself to hear to some inoffensive bit of psychopathy, which meant nothing except to the unfortunate subject.

"My dear fellow," I said, no mistrustfulness a little patronizingly," I'm sure you have not anything to confess that will make you out an outrageous devil, but if it'll do you any good to tell me your troubles, I'm ready to hear to them."

"Thank you," said Banaotovich in a pulsing voice." I have done nothing that they can put me behind the bars for. But I — I — —"

He goggled at me brutally.

"But I have done worse effects," he said solemnly," than some poor fellows that have been threaded up by the neck and choked to death!"

I laughed, a little nervously." Tell me your story, if you like," I said," and let me decide just how black you are. But I have not a great deal of apprehension. We are all of us poor miserable wrongdoers, as far as that is concerned. I could tell you effects about myself"

Banaotovich wasn't harkening to me at all. He'd fallen suddenly into a fit of black brooding. After a nanosecond or two, he looked up and asked sprucely

"Do you flash back Wolansky?"

Wolansky was the Greek professor who had hovered to bounce against Banaotovich when he was finishing his course at the Gymnasium.

" Of course," said I." And I flash back well how he abused you that lastyear. However, Wolansky was just that identical existent!"

If there ever was a dyspeptic old scoundrel." perhaps," he said absently; also after another pause

"Do you flash back that Wolansky failed suddenly, just a little while before the end of the academy time?"

I jounced." I imagine that was a great piece of good luck for you," I said.

" Yes," said Banaotovich. However, I should noway have had my parchment," If he'd lived. As it was, I finished withhonors. However, I'd have been ruined, If Wolansky had not failed when he did. Do not forget that — ruined!"

I was puzzled at his asseveration." Yes, you would have been seriously hindered," I agreed." Ruined is the word, maybe."

Banaotovich's face was grandiloquent with wine and some strange kind of suffering." Do you flash back another thing?" he said thickly." Do you flash back an old Hindoo who had a dark little hole down back of the shops and the beer depot and the livery forces between the Old Market and the swash?"

"The old fellow that had love charms and told fortunes and helped people to health and wealth and happiness?" I said in a tone of slightly forced gayness. It was hard to be cheerful with those dimmed eyes boring into you." Yes, I flash back him, each right. I wanted to go and see him formerly, when I was about fifteen or sixteen, but Father told me that poking with the black art had transferred further people to hell than it had helped. And Father was so terribly humorless about it that he frighted me. I noway went. As a matter of fact it was only a passing fancy, and I soon forgot each about him."

"That Hindoo," said my old academy- fellow courteously," knew effects about the secret forces in the macrocosm that made him nearly a god. And he tutored me effects that the wisest champion in the world does not questionable. Still, your father may have been right. I suppose it veritably probably that what he tutored me may shoot me to hell!"

I fiddled. I looked up nervously to make sure that the way was clear to the door. I began to suspect that my friend Banaotovich, though he was clearly not a felonious, might be a dangerous lunatic.

My vis- à- vis rubbed absently at a projection on his left side. I had noticed it when he first came across the room to speak to me. A disfigurement — I was sure it hadn't been there when he was a boy — or maybe a excrescence or some similar thing as that.

"I kept veritably quiet about what the Hindoo tutored me, because I knew utmost people felt about similar effects important as you say your father did. And I wanted to get on in the world. But I had an idea the Hindoo could help me get on. maybe he has"

And he goggled gloomily at space.

"Maybe he has. And maybe he hasn't."

He incubated. also he took up the thread of his story.

"Wolansky nearly drove me to self-murder. I read and studied and crammed, day and night. I tried everything I could suppose of to overcome the man's enmity. I crawled in the dust before him like a whipped dastard! Nothing did any good. And when I saw he abominated me and was determined to smash me, I began to detest him, too. I came to detest him worse than I abominated the devils in hell. There was a time when I had to hold myself back with all my strength to keep from sticking a cutter into him or braining him with a president. But the Hindoo and I made some trials with precognition, and I discovered that there are other ways of killing a man besides pecking him or giving him bane.

"I learned how to make a man in front of me on the road turn around and look at me. I learned how to make you conjure about me and come and tell me the dream the coming morning,"(when he said that, I jumped, for I flashed back having done exactly that thing!)." I learned how to bring out a bruise on Wolansky's face although he lived on the other side of city; so that he went around asking people how he could have banged his forepart without knowing it. And at last I went to bed one night, set my mind on Wolansky, and said over and over to myself a thousand times Die, you canine! You've got to die! I order you to die!

"I said it over till I fell into a kind of reverie . It was not sleep, I tell you. You can not sleep when you're in a state like that. And in my reverie , I could feel another arm grow out of my side then and grow longer and longer, and grow out through the window although the window was closed, and grow out across the road and down the road and right through the walls and across the swash.

"I had noway known where Wolansky lived. But that night I knew. I had noway known the road or the house number. I had noway been there in my life. But I can tell you just exactly how his bedroom looked. The marshland- stage between the two windows, the work- table against the west wall, the wardrobe, the old chesterfield against the north wall. In a corner the blue-argentine tiled cookstove with some of the pipe minced off. And against the south wall the bed he lay in. I can tell you the color of the mask he pulled up over his face. It was a dirty brownish red.

"But my hand sounded to go through the mask and grip Wolansky by the throat. First he soughed and turned his head to one side and tried to wriggle free. Also he raised his arms and tried to get hold of commodity that was not there. His sighs turned into groans, and the groans changed to a death rattle. He threw his arms and legs hectically around in the air, his body bent up like a arc. But my hand held his head down against the pillow. At last, he quit floundering and dropped down limp on the bed. Also the arm came crawling back in to my body, and I came out of the reverie — and went to sleep — or maybe I swooned.

"The coming morning the director came into our classroom and told us Wolansky had failed in the night of some kind of attack. You flash back that, I'm sure — —"

When Banaotovich began to tell me this story, he'd looked down from me, and his eyes noway met mine during the telling. He had begun with a painful trouble, but as he went on he grew more and more agitated and more and more inflamed with abomination of the vicious old Greek schoolteacher, till it nearly sounded as if he'd forgotten me and was living the astounding experience through for himself alone. When he was through, his elatedness of outrage left him and he sat dejected and alive, studying me pitifully out of the corners of his deep argentine eyes.

When he stopped speaking, there was a moment of silence. also I said commodity. I suppose what I said was," veritably extraordinary!"

He smiled, a simulated, sardonic smile." Extraordinary?" he repeated, with an interrogation point in his voice.

"Your jitters were strained to the breaking- point," I said." Your trouble with the old devil had driven you partial distracted. also there was all that occultistic hodgepodge with the old Hindoo. And you were trespassed and run down, anyway. No wonder you pictured dreams and saw fancies. And it may have been that there was some telepathic contact between you and Wolansky, and when he'd his apoplectic attack — —"

The sardonic smile strengthened on Banaotovich's face." So you have it all explained, and I am acquitted?" he inquired.

"Acquitted?" I cried." You were noway indeedaccused. However, the state would have a big job on its hands!"

If the state were to bring action against every man who had a feeling that he'd be happier if someone differently were out of the way." veritably true," Banaotovich consented icily." I see I have not got veritably far with you yet. You're forcing me to continue my not veritably edifying autobiography. — Did you know my father?"

I flashed back his father, and I flashed back that he hadn't enjoyed the stylish possible character.

"I suppose I knew him," I said hesitantly." He was a — a plutocrat- lender, was not he?

"Do not spare my passions," said Banaotovich plaintively." He was a usurer, and a cruel bone. I had a feeling for times that his business was a disgrace to the family, and I made no bones about telling him so. There were unattractive scenes. I allowed several times of leaving home. Eventually, Father told me one day that since I did not authorize of the way he got his plutocrat, he was doing me the favor of dispossessing me. I told him that was each right with me, that I'd rather starve than live on plutocrat that was stained with the blood of poor debtors.

I allowed at the time that I meant it. But about that time I had come interested in a youthful woman. I had noway had important to do with the girls, and veritably many of them sounded at all interested in me. But this bone appeared to like me, and when I made advances to her, she did not repel me. I'm no dilettante of womanish beauty, but I suppose she was surprisingly seductive, and at that time I was half frenetic about her. Still waters run deep, you know.

"Well, she had me under her spell so fully that I changed my mind about Father's plutocrat. I began to kowtow to him, much as I had toadied to Wolansky. I began to feel him out to find whether he'd made a will. He was veritably cold and indistinctive. Eventually I asked him outright if he'd review his decision to leave me poor. He told me it was I that had made the decision, not he, and that he'd no use for wishy-washy people that changed their minds like rainfall- cocks. He was veritably sardonic. I lost my temper and answered him back. We had a terrible quarrel, and eventually he — he struck me. I was twenty times old and a bigger man than he. And I suppose no man ever had further stubborn pride, at bottom, than I have.

"It was the Wolansky thing each over again. The demotion, the trouble at ingratiation, the failure, the long, eating, eating, growing abomination. And it — it ended the same way. The night of incubating that hardened into a devilish decision, the vision of the long arm, growing, stretching, crawling but not so far this time, only through two walls and across our own house. You flash back that Father failed of an apoplectic stroke, just as Wolansky had done a time or two ahead."

"Yes, I suppose I flash back ," I said in considerable embarrassment. The thing did begin to look uncanny. I was completely sorry for the poor, cracked fellow, but I would just as soon not have been alone with him in that solitary drinking- place in the twilight.

"Well?" he said, nearly sprucely.

" Well, Banaotovich," I answered with a show of confidence," you have had a great deal of unhappiness, and you have my sympathy. This strange faculty you have of anticipating deaths, like the night- owls and the death- watch that ticks in the walls, has made these misplacements an occasion of tone- torment for you. I suppose you should see a psychiatrist."

"Anticipating — anticipating?" Banaotovich had gone back and was repeating a word I had used, and as he repeated it he rapped madly on the table with his fritters." It's a curious coexistence that' anticipating' is just the word my woman used when I told her about it."

"You — told — your woman— What you have just told me?" I stammered." Do you suppose that was wise?"

"I could not help it," he said with a catch in his throat." I allowed I loved her, and I had to talk to notoriety. I was miserable, and I had a feeling that she might understand and be brought near to me by sympathy. Now that I suppose of it, I can see that I was an obvious idiot, but I discovered long ago that we are not rational beings after all. We're driven or drawn by mysterious forces, and we go to our destination because we can not help it.

"My woman had always sounded a little skittish with me. I noway sounded to have the gift of attracting people. And I do not know whether she'd ever have been interested in me at each if I had not used a little — a little charm the Hindoo tutored me. maybe that did not have important to do with it but I had noway been happy with her. Still that may be, one evening when she sounded surprisingly approachable, I had just the same impulse that I had when I met you then tonight, and I told her about Wolansky and Father. She pooh-poohed it all just as you did. But she was hysterical . I could see that. She was more and more hysterical of me as the days went by. For a long time she tried to be cordial and natural in my presence, but it was a sham and the poor thing could not keep it up. Each of us knew as well what was in the mind of the other as if we had talked the situation over honestly for hours. We reached the point where we could not look each other in the face. No solitariness could have been as ghastly as that solitariness of two people who participated a revolting secret. For I had induced her that I was shamefaced. I had succeeded in doing what I had set out to do, and I had ruined two lives in doing it. I've the faculty, it seems, of poisoning whatever I touch. Only moment, my woman said to me"

I started to my bases with a great rush of relief and appreciativeness." Ah, your woman is alive, also?" I cried.

"My woman is alive. That is my alternate woman is alive," he said, with a horrible forced smile.

I sank back heaving." What did you do with your first woman, you dirty hound?" I groaned in helpless outrage.

He closed his eyes, and a surge of bitter triumph played about the muscles of his mouth." Have I induced you too, at last?" he said.

Also I realized that I had been an insulting idiot. At worst, the man before me was a pathological case, and he clearly belonged in an shelter rather than in a captivity.

"Forgive me, Banaotovich," I gasped." I do not know what made me — —"

He looked at me sorely, nearly compassionately." There's nothing to forgive," he said, veritably still." I'm all you called me and a thousand times worse. Now let me finish my story."

"You do not need to," I said hastily." I know all the rest of it."

All interest, I'm hysterical nearly all sympathy, had gone out of me. What I wanted utmost of all was to get down from this melancholy citizen with power and madness in his argentine eyes.

" No, you do not know relatively all of it yet," he claimed." maybe if I tell you the whole story, indeed if you can not excuse me and I do not earn your excusing, I do not want your excusing you can understand me a little better, and suppose of me a little more kindly.

"There was another woman. I could not help it, any further than any of us can help anything. A fine, sympathetic youthful woman, who loved me because she knew I was unhappy. I had been married to the other woman for four times. We were fully disgruntled. We could scarcely bear to speak to each other. I could not be easy one moment in the same house with her. I had a hut in my office out in city because I could not indeed sleep soundly at home. It was hell. The terror in her eyes made me physically sick. My woman learned about the other woman. My woman was a devout Catholic, and there was no possibility of a divorce. I could read in my woman's face just what went on in her mind. She knew the other woman had come my only reason for living. And one day I read in her eyes, along with the terror, a glint of hopeless determination. She knew she was in peril, she knew I had a power that I could exercise when I chose in malignancy of all the courts and police and jails in the country. She knew her life was in peril, and her eyes told me that mine was in peril for that veritably reason. I did not condemn her. Half my grief through all the times had been grief for her. But the instinct of tone- defense in me was strong — and — she went — too — like — —"

"And she went, too, like the other."

He noway finished his judgment . He dropped his head on the table and began to cry hysterically. I laid a gingerly hand on his shoulder.

"Banaotovich," I said unsteadily," I am sorry for you — —"

He sat up and supported his chin in both hands." I have not been as — as bad as all this sounds like," he said after a while." Before I was married a alternate time, I went to the chief of police and gave myself up. The chief heeded to my story I did not try to explain it all, as I have done with you, but just blurted out the main data; but the longer he heeded the uneasier he came, and when I got through he asked me nervously if I did not suppose I ought to go into a sanitorium for a while. Also he bowed me out in a big hurry. maybe if I had told him all the sways and outs of it, it might have been different — —"

"But do not you suppose he is right about the sanitorium?"

"Right? I am as stable as you are. I have killed three people, a crazy scoundrel, a hard man, and a pure, innocent woman. But I did it all because I had to. A sanitorium wouldn't do me or anyone differently any good, and it would be a heavy expenditure. I've taken the responsibility for another pure, innocent woman, and I must support her. The war and the depression swept down my father's fortune, and my present business has downscaled down till I'm making only the barest living. I've applied for the agency for a big Berlin insurance company, and if I can get it, along with my other business, I shall be fairly comfortable. But I understand there's some talk of their transferring in a representative from outside. However, if they take the chuck out of my mouth like that, it will not be good for the stranger!"

If they do that. He was drunk, and his drunkenness was working him into an unattractive mood. He was dangerous, and physical courage was noway my strong point.

"What's the name of the Berlin Company?" I asked timidly.

He named the establishment I myself worked for. Also he fumbled for his bottle, and with stern and painful attention set about the delicate and delicate task of filling his glass again. I murmured commodity about being back in a moment, and made for the door. He was too busy to pay any attention to me.

When I had the door safely shut behind me, I dashed through the rain to my hostel as if the devil himself were after me.

It was a long time before I got over waking up in the middle of the night with the feeling that an icy, iron- muscled hand was clinging at my throat. I do not have the experience frequently any more, but I've noway seen the megacity of my birth since that awful night. I got out on the night train, and my company unwillingly gave me home on the other side of Germany.

Some time ago I happed to see a notice in the paper to the effect that a certain case named G. Banaotovich had failed suddenly in the Staatliche Nervenheilanstalt in Nuremberg. But I've met the name rather constantly of late, and I suppose it's a fairly common bone. I did not probe.

THE END

www.ingramcontent.com/pod-product-compliance
Lightning Source LLC
Chambersburg PA
CBHW080945120726
48003CB00011B/3298